Favourite Classics
A Little Princess

Retold by Sasha Morton
Illustrated by Andy Catling

An Hachette UK Company

www.hachette.co.uk

Copyright © Octopus Publishing Group Ltd 2013

First published in Great Britain in 2013 by TickTock,

an imprint of Octopus Publishing Group Ltd,

Endeavour House, 189 Shaftesbury Avenue,

London WC2H 8JY.

www.octopusbooks.co.uk

ISBN 978 1 84898 813 2

Printed and bound in China

10 9 8 7 6 5 4 3 2 1

With thanks to Lucy Cuthew

Contents

The Characters   4

Chapter 1   6
Sara Crewe

Chapter 2   12
Friends and Enemies

Chapter 3   18
The Birthday Party

Chapter 4   28
A New Life

Chapter 5   34
Princess of the Attic

Chapter 6   40
The Discovery

The Characters

Sara Crewe

Captain Crewe

Ram Dass

Mr Carrisford

At the School...

Miss Minchin

Miss Amelia

Becky

Ermengarde

Lavinia

Chapter 1
Sara Crewe

On a gloomy winter's day, many years ago, a little girl named Sara Crewe arrived in London.

She and her father had travelled there from

India so that Sara could go to boarding school.

"My darling, you will be very happy here," said her father. "Time will fly by and before you know it, you will be home with me again."

Their carriage pulled up outside a grand townhouse. Standing at the door was a tall, thin woman called Miss Minchin, who owned the boarding school.

Straight away, Sara did not like Miss Minchin.

Sara's father was to return to India, and as a gift, he had bought her a wardrobe of fine clothes and a doll named Emily. Sara and Captain Crewe sadly said their goodbyes.

"Oh, my little princess," said Sara's father fondly, "you have no idea how much I will miss you."

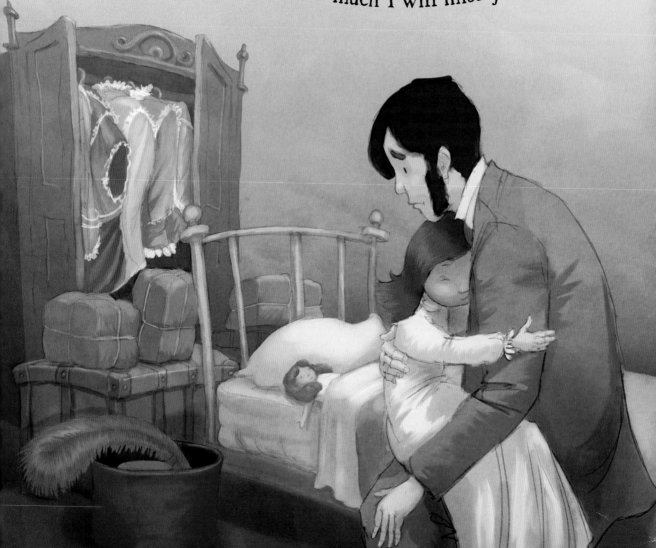

Sara waved from the
window until his carriage turned
the corner of the street and she was left alone.

Miss Minchin had arranged for Sara to occupy the biggest bedroom in the school. Miss Minchin explained to her sister, Miss Amelia, that Sara's father was very rich.

"She is to be treated like a princess.
This girl will make
me rich, too!"

9

On her first day of lessons, Miss Minchin called Sara to the front of the class to meet the French teacher.

"There really is no need for me to learn French," said Sara quietly.

"Sara, surely you do not think you can choose what you will learn here?" snapped Miss Minchin.

Keen to make herself understood, Sara turned to the teacher and spoke to him in perfect French. Miss Minchin's expression turned sour.

"Why, this child is right – she does not need lessons!" the teacher exclaimed.

Sara did not realise that she had embarrassed Miss Minchin. Unfortunately for her, the headmistress would not forget that in a hurry.

Chapter 2
Friends and Enemies

Until Sara had arrived, Lavinia had been the best-dressed girl in the school, and Lavinia was jealous that Sara had nicer clothes than her.

"I heard Miss Minchin say to Miss Amelia that her clothes were far too grand for a child of her age," said Lavinia nastily, throwing paper at Sara. "She isn't even pretty."

There was one girl who was always alone, who Lavinia and her friends laughed at. Sara found their behaviour cruel and so she invited the girl, called Ermengarde, to play in her room. From that moment on, Ermengarde and Sara were best friends.

Sometimes Sara was sad...

"Being without my father makes me unhappy," she explained.

"You and Emily make me feel better."

But when she was happy, Sara told wonderful tales about princesses and foreign lands, the likes of which Ermengarde could never have imagined!

Soon, more pupils started to go upstairs
to listen to Sara's
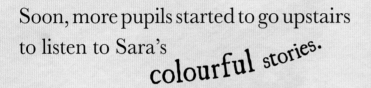
colourful stories.

While Lavinia bullied the smaller girls,
Sara would happily look after anyone
who hurt themselves or who needed
help with their schoolwork.

Lavinia grew
more
and
more
jealous
of Sara.

14

Meanwhile,
Miss Minchin could
not bring herself to like
Sara and grumbled to
Miss Amelia about the
strange, rich child. Miss Amelia thought her sister
was very unfair on Sara, but she would never have said so,
for Miss Minchin had **a terrible temper.**

Two years passed. One evening, as Sara told an exciting story to a group of pupils, she noticed the school's scullery maid listening too. Lavinia called out,

"The servant is listening!

How dare she?"

"It doesn't matter. Stories are for everyone,"

retorted Sara. But the girl had gone.

Sara was determined to make friends with the little servant girl and she did not have to wait long. The hard-working maid was so exhausted, she fell asleep in Sara's room that very evening!

"I'm so sorry, Miss! It won't happen again. **Please** don't tell Miss Minchin!"

Sara replied kindly,

"Of course I won't. It doesn't matter in the slightest. Stay and have some cake with me and tell me your name."

To the maid's astonishment, Sara talked to her just like she was any other girl in the school. That evening, the maid, Becky, crept back to the kitchen with a smile on her face for the first time.

Chapter 3
The Birthday Party

One day, a letter from Captain Crewe arrived.

My darling Sara,

An old friend, Tom Carrisford, has discovered that some land he owns contains real diamonds! Together we plan to mine for the gems and we will become very rich! What do you think of that, my little princess?

With all my love
as always,

Your Papa

Lavinia grumbled about Sara's growing wealth to her friends, saying,

"This is just another of Sara Crewe's silly stories. She already thinks of herself as a princess!"

Miss Minchin learned of the story and thought she could use it to her advantage. She decided to spare no expense in arranging Sara's eleventh birthday party.

If it became known that she was looking after a diamond heiress so well, she would surely get more rich girls at the school.

That would make her **rich** too!

One day Sara sneaked Becky a piece of cake, and Becky whispered, "I'll make sure to eat it quickly, to avoid leaving crumbs for the rats."

"Are there rats in your room?" gasped Sara, horrified.

"Plenty of mice and rats live in the attic, Miss," said Becky. "You get used to them after a while."

Sara looked around her beautiful bedroom. She couldn't imagine ever getting used to rats being near where she slept. She thought Becky was very brave. She felt very lucky to sleep where she did.

But thousands of miles away, all was not well. The worry over managing the diamond mine was making Captain Crewe ill.

Sara,
I am afraid I am not a very good businessman. The heat here makes it hard to think. You, with your wise ways, would probably be better at this than I!

Sara's **eleventh birthday** arrived. Miss Minchin had planned a huge party and bought piles of extravagant gifts for Sara.

She had even allowed the girls to finish lessons early to **celebrate!**

Just as Sara was cutting her birthday cake, there was a **knock** at the door.

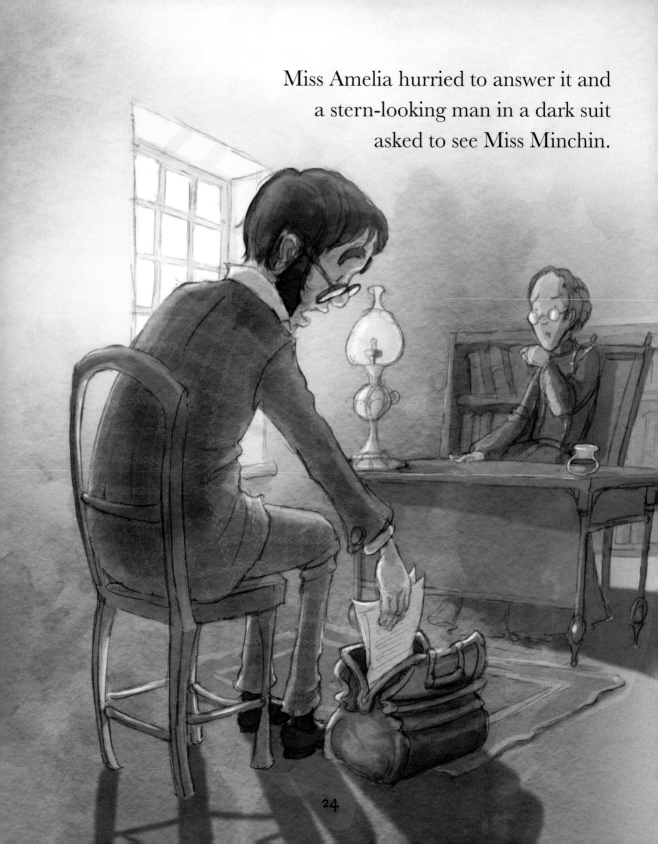

Miss Amelia hurried to answer it and
a stern-looking man in a dark suit
asked to see Miss Minchin.

The man had come to tell Miss Minchin of the Captain's death in India.

"I must also inform you that there is no money left in Captain Crewe's bank accounts," he said gravely.

Miss Minchin was very angry.
"Do you mean to tell me that Sara Crewe is a penniless orphan? I have just spent a small fortune on presents and a party for her!" she screeched.

Then she turned to her sister and said, "Find Sara Crewe and put her in a black dress. Her father is dead. Worse still, all her money is gone. The child is a pauper and apparently we must look after her! Bring her to me!"

In shock, Sara put on her old, too-small, black dress while whispering to herself,

"My papa is dead!"

Sara carried her doll, Emily, with her to Miss Minchin's study. The headmistress scowled at them both.

"You will have no time for dolls now."

Miss Minchin was furious. "I should throw you out onto the streets. But as an act of charity, I will let you stay here and work to repay your debts to me."

Sara said nothing, which made Miss Minchin even angrier. "Are you not going to thank me for giving you a home?" shouted the headmistress.

"This is not a home!" sobbed Sara. With that, she ran until she reached the attic where the other servants lived.

Becky crept into Sara's new bedroom.

"You see Becky," sobbed Sara. "I told you we were just the same, you and I."

"Whatever happens," wept Becky, "you will **always** be a princess."

Chapter 4
A New Life

Sara was put to work, carrying out all the usual cleaning jobs that a maid must do. But Miss Minchin heaped new duties upon her every day.

She taught the younger children French, helped them with their meals and heard their reading. She was sent on errands at all times and in all weathers and her working day became longer and longer.

Occasionally, she was allowed to take some old books into the schoolroom and study alone. **"One day, all of this will be different,"** Sara would think to herself as she tried not to fall asleep at the desk.

And at night, Sara would sleep in her broken bed, on a thin, lumpy mattress, and try not to listen to the sound of the rats in the rafters above her head.

Sara became thinner and more untidy looking as months passed by. The pupils almost forgot that she had ever been one of them. But not Ermengarde. Eventually one evening, Ermengarde plucked up the courage and crept up to the attic. Knocking on the door, she slipped into Sara's room.

"Miss Minchin doesn't want me to talk to the pupils," said Sara.

Then she had an idea.

"Perhaps you could creep up and pretend you are visiting a prisoner who has been held captive for years! Miss Minchin is the jailer and Becky is trapped in the cell next door."

The thought of playing a new pretend game with her old friend made Sara feel a little more like the girl who had lived downstairs, not so long ago.

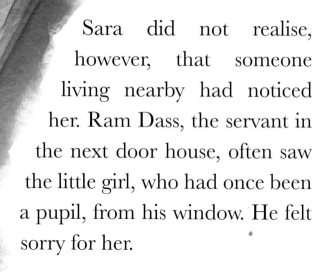

Sara did not realise, however, that someone living nearby had noticed her. Ram Dass, the servant in the next door house, often saw the little girl, who had once been a pupil, from his window. He felt sorry for her.

One evening, Ram Dass was in his own attic, when his pet monkey jumped across the rooftops and into Sara's room. When the skinny little maid handed back the monkey she spoke to him in Hindustani!

Ram liked her immediately.

By chance, Ram Dass was the servant of Tom Carrisford, the friend with whom Sara's father had gone into business. He too had fallen ill in India, and was now back in England recovering. As soon as he was well enough, Mr Carrisford intended to search for Sara Crewe as he had promised Captain Crewe he would find and look after his little princess.

Ram Dass told his master all about the little servant girl's cold, bare room.

"What if my poor old friend's daughter is living in the same terrible conditions?" Mr Carrisford wondered.

He decided he must set out on his search for his friend's daughter.

Chapter 5
Princess of the Attic

It was a harsh winter and Sara grew thin and tired. She was too proud to let Miss Minchin see her misery and Miss Minchin refused to show any kindness towards the girl who had once been her richest pupil.

One frosty morning outside the school, Sara spotted a coin lying on the ground. Excitedly, she decided to buy a bun for herself and Becky.

However, Sara noticed a family of beggars who looked even hungrier than she was.

The princess inside Sara rose up.

She went to the bakery and bought four buns.

Then, she gave them to the family.

When Sara arrived back at her attic room that night, the happy face of Ermengarde was waiting for her. But a moment later, Sara heard footsteps on the stairs. Miss Minchin stood in the doorway with a wicked smile on her face.

"So Lavinia was right!" she hissed. "What would Ermengarde's father say if he knew she was up here with a pauper like you?"

Sara looked at Miss Minchin and quietly replied, "I wonder what my father would say if he knew I was up here?"

Miss Minchin was speechless with rage. She ushered Ermengarde out and locked the door behind her.

The frosty attic really would be Sara's prison tonight.

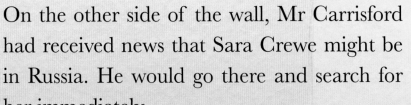

On the other side of the wall, Mr Carrisford
had received news that Sara Crewe might be
in Russia. He would go there and search for
her immediately.

While Ram Dass packed his
master's cases, he thought about
the servant girl in her lonely attic
and had an idea to help her, too.

Sara fell into a deep, exhausted sleep.
This allowed Ram Dass enough
time to creep in and carry out
his wonderful work.

A few hours later, a golden glow seemed to reflect off the walls of Sara's dirty attic and she felt warm in the lumpy bed. Opening her eyes, Sara couldn't believe what she was seeing.

"It's magic!" she whispered.

A fire crackled in the grate, food awaited her, and a dressing gown and slippers lay on the bed.

To the little girl in the attic.
From a friend.

Chapter 6
The Discovery

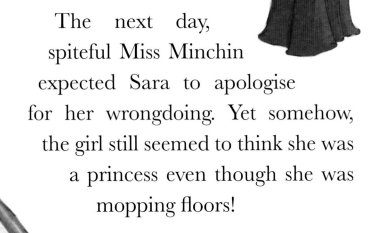

The magic that happened that night gave both Sara and Becky hope. They ate and drank until they were full and shared cosy new blankets between them.

The next day, spiteful Miss Minchin expected Sara to apologise for her wrongdoing. Yet somehow, the girl still seemed to think she was a princess even though she was mopping floors!

Life for Sara and Becky became more wonderful every day. Hot food awaited them in Sara's attic room in the morning and the evening.

Sara was even more surprised when a delivery boy arrived with a parcel addressed to 'The Little Girl in the Attic'. Inside was a pile of beautiful clothes and warm boots.

To be worn every day. Will be replaced by others when necessary.

Miss Minchin had no idea who Sara's mysterious benefactor could be but it was making the girl far too cheerful.

She did not like it at all.

A few weeks later, Sara heard a tapping on the roof. It was the monkey from next door! Sara let the monkey in to sleep and decided to return the tiny companion the next day.

The following afternoon, Mr Carrisford sat at his desk, sighing deeply. His journey to Russia had been a failure. The girl there was not Captain Crewe's missing daughter. He would have to start his search again, but where?

As the captain was thinking, Ram Dass interrupted him. "Sahib, the servant girl I have spoken of has returned the monkey. If it pleases you, I would like you to meet her."

Sara entered the room and curtsied to Mr Carrisford.

"I believe this is yours, Sir,"
she said politely.
"He reminds me of a monkey I owned
when I was a little girl in India."

Mr Carrisford looked
up at Ram Dass in
surprise as his servant
nodded wisely.

"What is your name, child?" asked Tom Carrisford, nervously.

"Sara Crewe, Sir," replied Sara.

Mr Carrisford gasped and then his words tumbled out in a rush. "Sara, your father invested in my diamond mine before the fever took him. Your father believed he was ruined."

"Were you the friend that kept me warm and fed?"
whispered Sara.

"No, that was Ram Dass. It seems he saw what I did not. That you are the lost heiress," smiled Mr Carrisford.

"I am no heiress, Sir.
    The money is all gone,"
            Sara said sadly.

Tom Carrisford smiled.
    "That is where you are
    mistaken, dear child. The mines
    were full of diamonds
    after all. You are rich, Sara."

Just then, they heard a gasp from the doorway. Miss Minchin had followed Sara and was ready to beat the girl for leaving the school without permission.

"Why, Sara, I was **SO** worried about you,"
said Miss Minchin.
"I've come to take you home."

"She is **not** going anywhere with you!"
replied Mr Carrisford sternly.

"But she belongs in my care! Her father..."
stuttered Miss Minchin in a panic.
If she lost Sara now she
would never be rich!

"In your 'care' she would
have starved to death," stated
Mr Carrisford. "Sara will be
staying with me, where she will
be treated like the princess that
she is."

"Oh, thank you!"
cried Sara happily.
"Thank you, both of you!"

When Miss Amelia
heard what had happened
she was glad for Sara. She had
had enough of her sister's wicked
ways, and bravely told her so.

"She was a good and clever girl and you
just hated that she acted like a princess
even when she was a servant!"

The other children were delighted
to see Miss Minchin thwarted.

That very day, Sara and Becky moved into the house next door. Nothing gave Miss Minchin – and Lavinia – less pleasure than seeing the girls who had once been servants living like princesses with Mr Carrisford. Ermengarde was a regular visitor to Sara's new home and they remained the best of friends. Most importantly, Sara was once more able to use her wealth to provide food to anyone in need…

believing everyone deserved the chance to have a life as happy as her own.